CASEY JONES'S FIREMAN
THE STORY OF SIM WEBB

NANCY FARMER PICTURES BY JAMES BERNARDIN

Casey

Sim

PHYLLIS FOGELMAN BOOKS • NEW YORK

To Fiona Rose N. F.
To my Seattle family, with love J. B.

Published by Phyllis Fogelman Books
Dial Books for Young Readers
A division of Penguin Putnam Inc.
345 Hudson Street
New York, New York 10014

Text copyright © 1999 by Nancy Farmer
Pictures copyright © 1999 by James Bernardin
Designed by Atha Tehon
Printed in Hong Kong on acid-free paper
First Edition
1 3 5 7 9 10 8 6 4 2

Library of Congress Cataloging in Publication Data
Farmer, Nancy.
Casey Jones's fireman: the story of Sim Webb/Nancy Farmer;
pictures by James Bernardin.—1st ed.
p.   cm.
Summary: Even though the railroad fireman senses danger ahead,
he follows his engineer's command to increase the train's power
so that the mysterious whistle blows.
ISBN 0-8037-1929-9
1. Jones, Casey, 1863–1900—Legends. 2. Webb, Sim—Legends. [1. Jones, Casey,
1863–1900—Legends. 2. Webb, Sim—Legends. 3. Afro-Americans—Folklore.
4. Folklore—United States.] I. Bernardin, James, ill. II. Title.
PZ8.1.F2225Cas 1999 398.2
[E]—DC20 95-12821 CIP AC

I was born a few yards from a railroad track. The trains rattled past my window every night, but they didn't frighten me. I thought the sound was a lullaby. I loved the railroad.

When I got older, my father sent me to school. I learned reading, writing, arithmetic, and bricklaying. Father thought bricklaying was a fine job. I preferred to sit on a wall and watch trains.

Some of the engines were crowned with antlers. Others had garlands of roses. In those days, engineers decorated their trains any way they liked. They had their own whistles too. I could tell by the music who was driving.

Fffollllowww meeee, the whistles called as they passed me on the wall. *Ssssiiiimmmm*, hissed the boilers in the engines.

I was put on earth to do something important. I don't think it's bricklaying, I decided.

I got a job with the railroad. In a short time I became a fireman. It was a hard and dangerous task. I shoveled coal into a red-hot furnace. I made sure water flowed into the boiler to make steam. If I made a mistake, the engine might explode, but I never made any mistakes. I was a good fireman, and soon I found myself working with Casey Jones, the best engineer in the country.

Casey could cut in front of a speeding train and never leave a scratch. He could shave an hour off a trip without even hurrying. But he was most famous for his whistle.

It had six quills, or pipes, fitted into a metal cup. It was powered by steam. When Casey pulled the whistle cord, children ran alongside the train. Cotton pickers put down their loads and smiled. The whistle blew until it rattled the pearly gates of heaven. I saw the angels leaning over the clouds to listen.

One evening Casey and I were strolling along the streets of Memphis, Tennessee. We were going to drive the *Cannonball* Express that night. As we passed a saloon, someone shouted, "Casey! Casey!"

I frowned. I didn't like saloons.

"Casey, my lad!" A gentleman with bristly red hair and sideburns stood in the doorway. He had a flushed face, as though he had been standing too close to a fire. "I hear you have a six-quill whistle on your train."

"Yes, sir," Casey replied politely.

"I have a *seven*."

I knew that wasn't possible. No one had a seven-quill. The more pipes you had, the more steam you needed to blow all of them. And that much steam was dangerous.

"Show me," said Casey. So the red-haired gentleman took us into an alley. He had a wagon pulled by a big, black horse that rolled its eyes when it saw me.

The gentleman unpacked the whistle. Six of the pipes were plain, but the seventh—and longest—was marked with a pattern of flames. *And the whole thing was made of gold.*

"I could never afford that," Casey said.

"I'll let you borrow it," said the gentleman.

"Oh, no, sir! Every outlaw in the country would be on my tail."

"Listen, no one can steal *this* whistle." The gentleman bent close and whispered, "It's made from the angel Gabriel's trumpet. The Bible says it's the very one he's supposed to blow on Judgment Day."

"If it's Gabriel's trumpet, how did *you* get it?" I asked.

The red-haired gentleman ignored me. He raked his long, curved fingernails across the quills. The golden pipes rang like bells.

"Oh!" cried Casey as though he had been struck.

The sweet spring air of Memphis shivered with the most heavenly chord. It slowly died away until I could almost see the crack where it slipped out of sight.

"Gabriel's trumpet belongs to the angels," I said. "People don't have any business using it."

"I'm only borrowing it, Sim. Gosh! Can you see the faces of the other engineers when I blow it? They'll think the end of the world has come!" Nothing could stop Casey after he heard that heavenly chord. He proudly carried the whistle to the station. I followed with a bad feeling inside.

The *Cannonball* was being gussied up for her night run. We fitted the seven-quill whistle in place.

"Ain't that something? The old girl's got a new crown," Casey said. The gold shone like a star above the smoky hide of the engine. The pattern of flames seemed to writhe in the dim light.

The clouds were low and heavy when we started out, but Casey was in a fine mood. He touched the whistle cord. Heads snapped around. Porters dropped their bags. Casey laughed and drove on in a cloud of steam.

We flew along the tracks with a roll that only the best trains driven by the best men can achieve. Now and then Casey pulled the cord: *Caaaaseeeey Joooooones*, said the whistle over the dark cottonfields and shanty houses. Farmers stumbled out of bed, horses kicked in stalls, roosters flapped to the tops of henhouses.

Casey blew the first, second, and third of the golden pipes. As the train speeded up, he played the fourth and fifth. The boiler hissed. Red flames licked out along the side of the engine. Casey blew the sixth pipe, but try as he would, he couldn't get enough power to play the seventh. "I need more steam. Lay on more coal," he yelled.

"We're going too fast already," I shouted.

"Don't you tell me how to run a train!"

"Mr. Casey, we have a hundred passengers on board."

"Darn you! Lay on more coal!" he yelled again.

So I did, although I thought it was a bad idea.

Leaning back in his seat, Casey was as happy as a king. "Oh, Sim! The old girl's got her high-heeled slippers on tonight!"

What was it about that whistle, I thought as the sweat rolled off my back. Once you played the first pipe, you *had* to do the rest. It was like a craving for strong drink. And what happened when you got to the seventh?

Suddenly, sure as anything, I knew what would happen. That really *was* Gabriel's trumpet! When Casey blew the seventh pipe, all the farms and cities and mountains and oceans would go to glory. The world would end! And it wasn't the right time yet!

I stopped shoveling coal. I leaned out the side and saw two red lights ahead. It was another train on the track! "Look out, Mr. Casey!" I shouted.

Casey yanked on the brake handle with all his strength. The wheels clamped down. The smell of hot metal filled the air. The red lights loomed up ahead as big as houses.

"Jump, Sim!" Casey shouted. I leaned out the side and let go. I hit the dirt with a bone-rattling crash. I rolled over and over down the slope.

Casey pulled the train up like a cowboy hauling in a wild horse. The brakes screamed; sparks flew off the tracks. He slowed the engine by half in those last seconds, but it wasn't enough. I heard a terrible crash as I landed in a tangle of bushes.

They found Casey with his hand still on the brakes. The caboose of the train ahead was shattered; the next two cars had burst open, scattering hay and corn everywhere. But no one else had been killed. Casey had saved the lives of all the other people.

I found the gold whistle in the weeds. It wasn't even dented. It was all ready to tempt another engineer. "I was put on earth to do something important," I said. "I believe I'll keep this whistle somewhere safe."

When I retired, I gave the whistle to another fireman, who later passed it on to a brakeman, who gave it to an engineer.

One day Gabriel himself will show up at the door of an old railroad man's house. He'll tell him to fire up the boiler and play that whistle until it rattles the pearly gates of heaven.

Lay down your tools, you working men and women, Gabriel will cry. *It's time to go home. You've earned a nice, long vacation.*

Casey and I and all the other angels will dance on the clouds. Because then it will be the *right* time for Gabriel's trumpet to blow.

Sim Webb and **Casey Jones** were real people. The sentence about the high-heeled slippers is from Sim's autobiography. In the last minutes before the crash, Casey slowed the *Cannonball* down from seventy miles an hour to about forty. Sim jumped when it was going fifty.

In Sim Webb's day there was no special school for learning how to run a train. Teenaged boys would sometimes work for nothing in the hope of catching an engineer's eye. Then they would learn each chore on the job. Sim Webb had a slight edge because his father already worked for the railroad as a carpenter.

It was a great accomplishment in 1895 for a black man to advance as far as fireman. A fireman was second only to the engineer and was qualified to run the train on his own if it became necessary.

In the nineteenth century, engineers decorated their own trains. They had personal handmade whistles. Casey's was famous for its haunting whippoorwill call. It now belongs to his grandson.

Engines and trains had names in the same way as ships. *Hercules*, *General Grant*, and *Gunpowder* were typical engine names. The names were usually masculine, although one train was called *Mrs. Duston*, after a woman who was abducted by a band of Iroquois in 1699. She returned home after killing ten of them and collecting their scalps.

Trains might be called *The Aztec Eagle* or *City of New Orleans*. Several were named *The Cannonball*. The train Casey Jones drove was the pride of the Illinois Central Railroad. The accident occurred in 1900 when Casey was thirty-six and Sim was twenty-five.

Sim retired in 1919. He wasn't strong enough to do the job of fireman anymore. He went back to bricklaying, but always missed the railroad.

N. F.